ISBN-13:978-1539008361
ISBN-10:1539008363

For Richard,

From one sparkly diamond to another,

thank you for helping me to find my shine

Love Nicky
xx

Acknowledgements

I have spent my lifetime with my head in a book, from story books to autobiographies, to text books and now therapy books. Their ability to remove us from the world and allow us to enter new realms and lands, to absorb ourselves in characters and plots has kept me engrossed since childhood. Through my early career I would recite children's books to my early year's children quickly, slowly, loudly and quietly, sharing pictures and words. Every moment leading to this one, right here. So it is important to give thanks to those who have supported that love of words which led me to the creation of the Adventures of Brian Books.

To Mum, thank you for sharing stories with us as children, teaching us to read and, when we were old enough to read for ourselves, ensuring we always had a stock of books to satisfy those literacy needs. Dad, thank you for your safari stories when we were young, entrancing us in your adventures, inspiring an imagination.

To Richard for your belief and encouragement, and most of all for inspiring me from the moment I met you, to have met a fellow book and word lover has propelled me forward in my writing, opening my eyes, I thank you from the bottom of my heart for your guidance in finding my shiny diamond.

To my nan and granddad, who forever guide me to follow this path that I am on and to ensure that I stay true to my dreams.

To Veronica, thank you for allowing me the privilege of naming Brian after Brian. A man we all loved and whose love keeps us moving forward every day.

To Elise, Darcey & Boo, thank you to my 'other' family for your ongoing support, thank you to Darcey for your love of my stories and to Elise for your support, being an ear to listen on our many walks with Brian and Boo. Thank you to Boo for being the best friend Brian could ask for.

To Gemma, thank you for always demonstrating kindness and loving Brian with all your heart.

I hope you enjoy these books as much as I have enjoyed writing them

Love Nicky x x

HELPING CHILDREN OVERCOME THEIR FEARS AND WORRIES

This book belongs to:

....

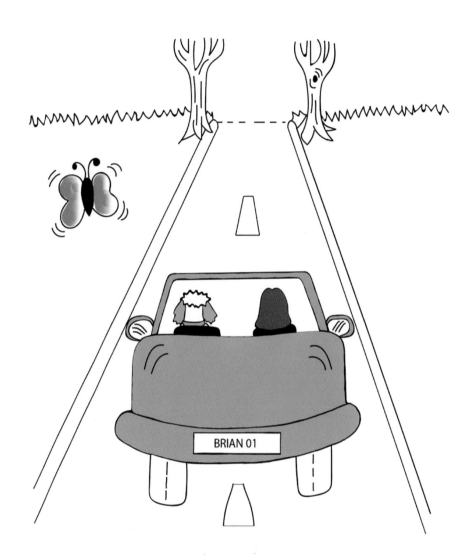

Today Brian is feeling a little bit sad, Brian was worried and he didn't really know why? His mummy said they were going for a walk to the forest which made him feel a little bit happier, when he was with her he always felt better.

They jumped in the car and his mummy drove them to the forest. When they got there Brian looked at the beautiful trees and saw the birds flying through the sky. He loved it in the forest, it was one of his favourite places!

They walked around the forest, through the trees …. Brian jumped in the piles of leaves and rolled in them. He ran through the long grass like a little lion and round the beautiful lake with the ducks on it. Brian loved to smell everything, he especially loved to sniff everything in the forest as the leaves, the trees and the flowers smelt so good! Today Brian decided to sniff for treasure in the forest!

He followed his nose between the trees, through the grass and around the lake. He was so busy following his nose that his mummy had to call him to remind him not to end up in the lake! Brian secretly thought it would be a little bit funny to get all wet and soggy, but he didn't think his mummy would find it funny!

The sun was shining and as Brian sniffed the leaves he smelt a nice smell.... So he followed it, every now and again he looked over his shoulder to make sure his mummy was following though!

He kept sniffing and soon he came to a huge tree! The trunk was so wide Brian had to run really fast to get around it! The branches reached so far into the sky Brian had to stretch his neck so that he could see them! In the top of the tree he could see a squirrel sitting watching him.

Brian sniffed around the tree roots, then he rolled in the leaves, kicking his feet in the air, the leaves tickled his back – he liked that!

All of a sudden he felt something!

Brian rolled over and used his paws to dig through the leaves, and there, under the leaves he found a round, black pebble!

Brian laid down and looked closely at the black pebble…. It was a little bit shiny and an oval shape.

Brian looked at it a bit more… the pebble was very pretty, he could see his reflection in it! Brian decided that this pebble was the treasure he needed to find. He decided to take it home so he picked it up in is mouth and carried it back to the car!

When he got home he hid it in his bed, as he knew his mummy would try to put it in the garden but he knew he needed to look after it!

He tucked it under his blanket so that she wouldn't see it (and did a little giggle to himself at how clever he was) and then ran off to play in the garden until his lunch was ready.

After he had eaten his lunch Brian went back to his bed to play with his pebble…. He was a little bit surprised to discover that it was a little bit more shiny than it had been earlier.

As you know, if you look after things then they stay like new, but Brian had never seen a pebble become more shiny before!

That night Brian curled up in his bed with his black shiny pebble and fell fast asleep…. As he slept the pebble became a little bit warmer….

As you know when we are loved and cared for we all feel warmer inside… and as Brian slept with the pebble under his blanket that night it seemed that the pebble was the same!

When Brian woke up the next morning he jumped out of bed and looked at the pebble. It was even shiner! Brian had kept the pebble warm all night and it seemed that the pebble was changing! Brian's black pebble was now prettier than before!

Now, you probably already know, that when we keep warm we feel better, and Brian's pebble seemed to like it too! That day Brian took his pebble everywhere!

He took it in the garden when he played ball!

He laid with it when he had a nap!

He showed it to his friend the Blue Butterfly!

He sat with it when he ate his favourite treat!

He even held it in his paws while his mummy brushed his hair!

At the end of the day when he went to bed Brian placed the pebble back under his blanket and as he fell asleep Brian realised that he felt really happy.

The next morning Brian was excited to see what his pebble was like! He jumped out of bed and pulled back the blanket and when he looked at his black pebble he discovered that it had changed colour!

Brian's black shiny pebble was now grey and shiny! Brian looked at it and tilted his head... the pebble had been with him all night and he couldn't believe his eyes that now the pebble was grey!

He pushed it with his paw.... It was warmer too! Brian was even more excited! This pebble was really magic!

That day Brian was going on a walk with his Nanny and Granddad so he took his pebble too, he carried it in his mouth the whole way so that it was safe. They had a lovely day, they saw the flowers, walked round the pretty lake and watched the ducks. Brian had the best day he felt so happy and his tail wiggled really, really fast!!

When Nanny and Granddad dropped him home he was so tired, he ran into his house with his pebble and jumped into his bed.

As he dropped his pebble on the blanket he looked at it closely....

The pebble was an even lighter grey! And when Brian touched it with his nose he realised that it was toasty warm, all snuggly! As Brian snuggled up with his pebble for a little nap he felt all warm and cosy.

The next morning it was sunny outside so Brian picked up his pebble and took it into the garden. He sat the pebble on the grass and ran around the garden. He played in the flowers and watched his friend the Blue Butterfly fly though the sky.

He showed Blue Butterfly his pebble and told her how it had changed colour

"You know, if you look after things then they become more special, don't you?" said Blue Butterfly

Brian looked at Blue Butterfly and then looked at the pebble "You're right Blue Butterfly, I will take extra special care of my pebble" he said

"You might find, that when you look after it, it will make you feel happier too" said Blue Butterfly, then she fluttered her wings and flew into the sky……

Brian thought about what Blue Butterfly had said, he had taken care of the pebble and shown it lots of his favourite things, the more he took care of it, the prettier it became. The more he took care of it, the happier Brian felt.

That night as Brian went into the house for dinner he went to pick up his pebble and realised that there were lots of little sparkles all over it!

Brian smiled, Blue Butterfly was right, the more you look after things the better they become!

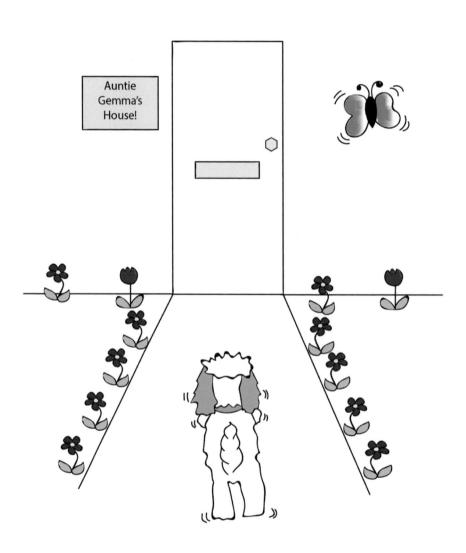

The next day his mummy was taking him to Auntie Gemma's house! Brian loved his Auntie Gemma because she gave him big cuddles and played with him, she always made him feel happy.

Just as he was about to go to the car he remembered his pebble! He dashed back into the house, even though his mummy was calling, he picked up his pebble and ran back to her.

As they sat in the car Brian licked the pebble to make sure it was nice and clean to show his Auntie Gemma. His mummy tried to take it off him but he sat on it so she couldn't get to it!

When they got to Auntie Gemma's house he jumped out of the car and ran to her door! She was very happy to see him! Brian was very happy to see her too! He ran into the living room, jumped on the sofa and hid his pebble behind the cushion so that they wouldn't find it. That afternoon Auntie Gemma tickled his tummy and threw his ball, he had the best day!

When it was time to leave he remembered his pebble and jumped up on the sofa to get it, when he pushed the cushion on the floor to get it he found that his pebble was completely white and sparkly!

'Wow thought Brian – my pebble is so beautiful! The more I look after it the better it becomes!'

Brian was so very sleepy when they got home that he wandered into his bed, he popped his white sparkly pebble under his blanket and fell fast asleep!

That night Brian had the nicest dreams! He dreamt of running in the field with Boo, having tummy tickles with Auntie Gemma and playing ball with Nanny and Granddad... all his favourite things!

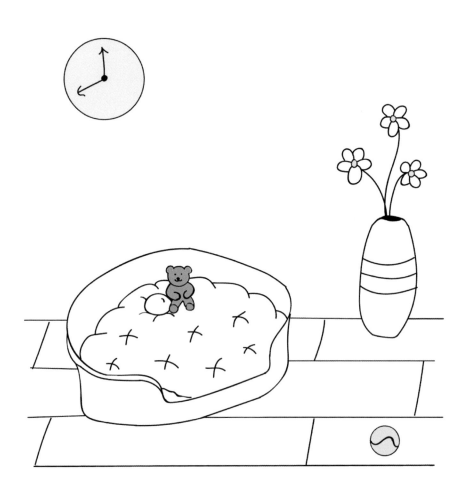

When he woke up the next morning he pulled off the blanket to check his pebble was still white and sparkly! It was! Brian was so excited! He remembered what Blue Butterfly had said…. "If you look after things then they become more special"

Brian knew that Blue Butterfly was right, he had looked after his black pebble and the more he cared for it and did nice things with it, the better it became….Doing nice things made him happy as well!

Today Brian was going for a walk with his best friend Boo! Brian loved to run round and play chase with her!

Brian decided that he should leave his pebble at home though, he would tell Boo about it when they ran, but he didn't want to lose it (the field was very big) so he popped it in his bed with his favourite bear to keep it safe.

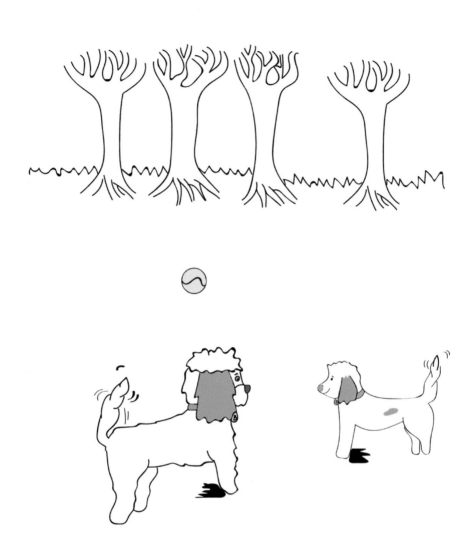

Boo and Brian ran round the field, they were so fast! Brian chased Boo and then Boo chased Brian! They rolled in the grass and while they laid in the grass Brian told Boo about his pebble.....

"So, it was black and now its white and sparkly?' asked Boo

"Yes! It's like magic! When I found it I looked after it, took it to places that made me happy and now it's white and sparkly!" said Brian!

"Hmm.... Is it magic?" asked Boo

"Maybe, but I was thinking, when our mummies look after us it makes us feel better doesn't it?" said Brian to Boo

"Yes definitely! When our mummies take us for walks, feed us and spend time doing nice things with us I always feel happy" said Boo

"Well, I was thinking, when you look after things they become happier and better! So that must be what happened to my pebble too!" said Brian

That night Brian went to bed and looked at his pebble, it was still white and shiny! He thought about what he and Boo had talked about.

When you look after things they really DO feel better….. When he played with his doggie friends it made him feel happier and braver, when he spent time with his mummy he felt warm inside, and when he did things he liked, like run around the field with Boo he always felt so happy.

With those happy thoughts he fell asleep with his paw on his pebble…. That night while Brian was asleep the pebble changed one last time….

When Brian woke up the next morning he had a shiny diamond in his paw! It was the most beautiful thing that he had ever seen!

"Wow" said Brian!

He sat looking at it, he tilted his head to the left, and he tilted his head to the right as he looked at the beautiful shiny diamond in his paw…. His black pebble had turned into the most beautiful thing he had ever seen…

Then Brian thought about how…. even though the diamond was sparkly and beautiful he had loved the black pebble just as much… The diamond was prettier than the pebble but it did not mean that the pebble was not as special….

But the pebble had turned into the sparkly diamond because Brian had taken good care of it!

Looking after his pebble had also made Brian feel braver and happier than ever before! It was just like the Blue Butterfly had told him:

"If you look after things then they become more special"

Blue Butterfly was right! When you take care of things they grow more special, just like his pebble!

As Brian sat looking at his pebble he saw Blue Butterfly flutter past the window… He jumped up and ran outside with his pebble to show her!

Brian and the Blue Butterfly watched the diamond shine in the sunlight and Brian said to Blue Butterfly

"Do you know what Blue Butterfly? When we take care of things and people then it makes us feel better?'

"I did" said Blue Butterfly, "When we look after people and ourselves it gives us confidence and it means that we feel happier when we do things"

"Since I have had my pebble and now my diamond, I feel better" said Brian

"That's because you found the things that make you happy Brian" said Blue Butterfly! Then they ran and fluttered round the diamond and had a lovely morning in the sunshine.

Sometimes the most beautiful things and people we meet are like that black pebble, we just need to love and care for them and then they can shine!

Other books in this series:

Brian and the Blue Butterfly

Brian and the Magic Night

Brian and the Black Pebble

Nicky lives in Sussex with Brian the Cockapoo where they enjoy daily adventures with friends and family. Nicky started her career by spending 10 years working in the early years sector with 0-5 year olds before lecturing in early years and health and social care to students aged 16 and over. She later retrained as a hypnotherapist and now runs A Step at a Time Hypnotherapy working with children and adults to resolve their personal issues.

The Adventures of Brian books were the development of a dream of wanting to offer parents of young children tools and resources to support their children to manage worries and fears in a non-intrusive way. Having spent a large part of her career reading stories at all speeds and in all voices this collection of storybooks was born.

Each book in the collection covers a different worry which affects children on a day to day basis and uses therapeutic storytelling to support children in resolving these through Brian's daily adventures.

You can find more titles in the Adventures of Brian series by visiting:

www.adventuresofbrian.co.uk

16044885R00027

Printed in Poland
by Amazon Fulfillment
Poland Sp. z o.o., Wrocław